When I Wear My Tiara

By Lisa Lebowitz Cader   •   Illustrated by Laura Huliska-Beith

chronicle books · san francisco

When I wear my tiara,
I reign over my kingdom and get
to make all the rules.

When I wear my tiara,
I have vast knowledge
at my fingertips.

When I wear my tiara,
I tour my lands in a royal carriage.

When I wear my tiara,
I outwit foes with ease.

When I wear my tiara,
I make peace among
warring knights.

When I wear my tiara,
I dance beautifully at the ball.

When I wear my tiara,
I am kind and loving to all
my subjects.

When I wear my tiara,
I am brave enough to
face anything.

When I wear my tiara,
I rest easily in my bedchamber,
knowing I have ruled well.

Book design by Charles Kreloff.
Typeset in Hank.
The illustrations in this book were rendered in
mixed media of acrylic and paper/fabric collage.
Manufactured in China.

Distributed in Canada by Raincoast Books
9050 Shaughnessy Street, Vancouver, British Columbia V6P 6E5

10 9 8 7 6 5 4 3 2 1

Chronicle Books LLC
85 Second Street, San Francisco, California 94105

www.chroniclekids.com